This book belongs to:

_____

_____

_____

First published 2008 by Walker Books Ltd
87 Vauxhall Walk, London SE11 5HJ

This edition published 2012

2 4 6 8 10 9 7 5 3 1

© 2008 Lucy Cousins
Lucy Cousins font © 2008 Lucy Cousins

The author/illustrator has asserted her moral rights
Illustrated in the style of Lucy Cousins by King Rollo Films Ltd
Maisy™. Maisy is a registered trademark of Walker Books Ltd, London

Printed in China

British Library Cataloguing in Publication Data:
a catalogue record for this book is
available from the British Library

ISBN 978-1-4063-4459-2

www.walker.co.uk

Maisy Goes to the Museum

Lucy Cousins

WALKER BOOKS
AND SUBSIDIARIES
LONDON · BOSTON · SYDNEY · AUCKLAND

One rainy day Maisy went to the museum with her friends.

They all like the museum very much.

First everyone wanted to see the dinosaur. What enormous bones! And look at the fossilised dinosaur's egg!

EGG

T-REX

In the transport section, Charley loved the vintage car...

and the penny farthing bicycle...

and the
double-decker bus!

What a wonderful old biplane! And look here, a satellite, and a rocket!

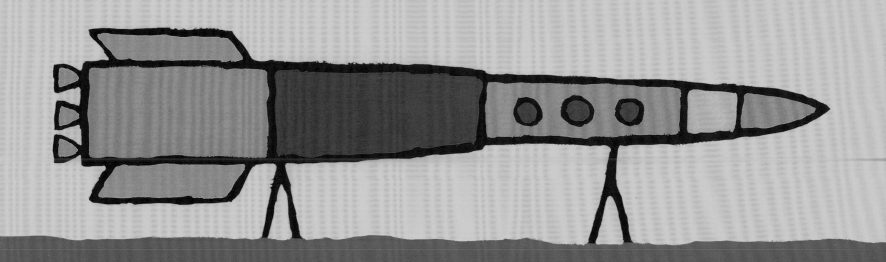

Maisy imagines being an astronaut and flying to the moon with Panda.

Everyone enjoyed
the old toys.

Tallulah's favourite
was the grand
doll's house with
all its tiny
furniture.

In the natural history section, Maisy and Charley marvelled at the brightly coloured birds.

INSECTS

Tallulah inspected the insects.

Cyril made friends with
the sabre-toothed tiger.

And Eddie looked and looked at the dear old woolly mammoth.

There's so much
to see and do
at the museum.

You can draw...

play with
puppets...

make music...

and dress up in the costume room. Maisy dressed up as an Egyptian.

Cyril was a knight.
Look at his shining armour.

"Now it's time to visit the food section!" Charley said.

So they went to the museum café and had delicious cakes and refreshing drinks.

"There's always something new to see at the museum," Maisy said on the way home.

"And there's always something old to see," said Eddie.

My friend Maisy

Maisy Goes to Bed

Lift the flaps! Pull the tabs!

A Maisy Classic Pop-up Book Lucy Cousins

ISBN 978-1-4063-0970-6

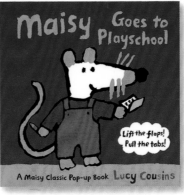

Maisy Goes Swimming

Lift the flaps! Pull the tabs!

A Maisy Classic Pop-up Book Lucy Cousins

ISBN 978-1-4063-0972-0

Maisy Goes to Playschool

Lift the flaps! Pull the tabs!

A Maisy Classic Pop-up Book Lucy Cousins

ISBN 978-1-4063-0971-3

Maisy Goes to the Playground

Lift the flaps! Pull the tabs!

A Maisy Classic Pop-up Book Lucy Cousins

ISBN 978-1-4063-0976-8

Maisy at the Farm

Lift the flaps! Pull the tabs!

A Maisy Classic Pop-up Book Lucy Cousins

ISBN 978-1-4063-0973-7

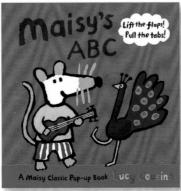

Maisy's ABC

Lift the flaps! Pull the tabs!

A Maisy Classic Pop-up Book Lucy Cousins

ISBN 978-1-4063-0974-4

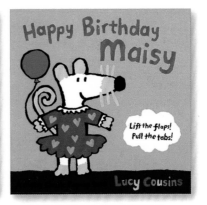

Happy Birthday Maisy

Lift the flaps! Pull the tabs!

Lucy Cousins

ISBN 978-1-4063-0691-0

It's more fun with Maisy!

Available from all good booksellers